AND THE
DEADLY
GLADIATORS

PaRragon

Bath · New York · Singapore · Hong Kong · Cologne · Delhi · Melbourne

Written by Zed Storm
Creative concept and story by E. Hawken
Words by Rachel Elliot
Check out the website at www.will-solvit.com

First edition published by Parragon in 2010

Parragon
Queen Street House
4 Queen Street
Bath BA1 1HE, UK

Copyright © Parragon Books Ltd 2010

ISBN 978-1-4075-8984-8

Printed in China

Please retain this information for future reference.

CONTENTS

"When was Julius Caesar murdered?" asked Zoe.

"Who cares?" I growled.

We were revising for a school history test on ancient Rome, and I was fed up. OK, so homework's never exactly fun, but this felt like rubbing salt into a wound. It felt like ages since my last Adventure.

I come from a long line of Adventurers, and I had already got into the habit of sort of expecting Adventures to happen. I mean, anyone who keeps getting mysterious letters from an unknown writer should always be on the lookout for Adventures, right?

Wrong.

The last letter had told me that I'd be travelling back in time to ancient Rome. But that had been two weeks ago, and I hadn't had a sniff of an Adventure. This history test on ancient Rome was the last straw. I was pinning all my hopes on finding my mum in ancient Rome. The test was just making me feel sick and miserable.

Mum and Dad had been missing in time since a mix up in a prehistoric jungle. I had tried to find them, but my dad's most amazing invention, Morph, wasn't exactly reliable. The time machine chip didn't always work, and it certainly didn't always take me where I wanted to go.

I had tried for two weeks to get Morph to take me to ancient Rome, and what was the result? Morph was willing to turn into a laptop, an electric guitar or even a tumble dryer, but a time machine? In my dreams.

Can't find Mum and Dad with a guitar!!

8

My best mate, Zoe, was busily making notes and flipping through textbooks. She had got a 'B' for her last essay, which was like Zoe's worst nightmare. It had totally brought out her competitive side. She was determined to pass this test with the highest marks in the class.

I read the paragraph on Mark Antony for the fifth time, sighed and reached for a lime-and-jelly-baby biscuit. Grandpa had gone shopping, but before going he had made some snacks to help me and Zoe through the revision. We had polished off the peanut-butter-and-olive fritters, but we were taking our time with the biscuits, and we hadn't even dared to try the kipper-and-onion muffins yet.

In my mind I went over everything I knew about ancient Rome:

1. The ancient Roman Empire was one of the biggest empires ever.
2. Ancient Romans spoke Latin.
3. They believed in a whole load of gods and goddesses.
4. Only citizens could wear togas. Foreigners and slaves were forbidden to wear them.
5. The Roman Emperor wore laurel leaves on his head instead of a crown.
6. Slaves were trained as gladiators and fought for public entertainment.

"OK, let's test each other and see if we know everything," said Zoe, her eyes shining with the light of competition. "I'll start. What was the ancient name for France?"

"Gaul," I muttered through gritted teeth.

At that moment I resented everything I had

My board is sooo cool!!

to learn about ancient Rome. I didn't want to be reading about it – I wanted to be there!

"What was a gladiator's average lifespan?"

"Does it really matter to you that much?" I snapped.

Zoe slammed her textbook shut and forced a grin onto her face.

"I know why you're in a bad mood, so I'm going to try really hard not to react," she said. "Let's take a break from revising. Fancy doing a bit of boarding?"

I smiled for the first time all morning.

"You read my mind!"

Five minutes later we were in the garden with our skateboards under our arms. Actually, 'garden'

doesn't really describe the area around Solvit Hall, Grandpa Monty's house. I had been living there ever since Mum and Dad disappeared, and I still managed to get lost in the grounds most days. It'd take hours to walk around the garden, and that isn't even counting the football pitch, the tennis courts, the aeroplane runway or the helicopter-landing pad.

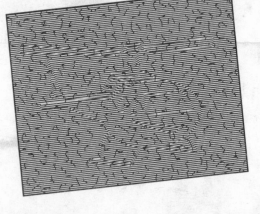

We chose an area where there was a lot of open space without bushes or trees to get in our way. I activated Morph's skate ramp program, and within seconds the grass was hidden underneath a huge ramp.

"That is so cool," said Zoe.

She hopped onto her skateboard and took off. I watched her for a while before joining in. Zoe is a brilliant skater, and when she's really blasting, her board just looks like it's part of her.

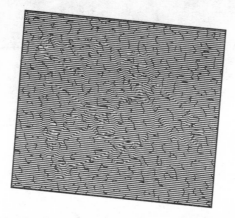

I feel kind of proud of that board – I made it while I was in the Stone Age and taught my caveboy friend, Ned, how to skate. But that's a whole other story!

We had been skateboarding for about half an hour when something caught my eye. It was a brownish-yellow envelope sitting on one of Grandpa Monty's prize topiary bushes (they're the ones you can trim into funny shapes). This particular bush was currently shaped like a giant peacock. Distracted, I lost control of the board and careered off the ramp into the bush.

From inside the peacock-shaped bush I heard Zoe shriek, and then I felt her hands gripping my ankles. My hands were trapped and I couldn't move, but Zoe pulled so hard that I shot out like a cork from a bottle and landed with a bump on her stomach.

"Get off me, you big lump!" she wheezed.

I stood up and rubbed my hair, which was full

of small twigs, tiny green leaves and beetles. Zoe jumped to her feet.

"I've never seen someone who really has been dragged through a hedge backwards before," said Zoe, staring at me with interest. "What made you decide to go in for hedge diving? It's not an Olympic sport, you know."

"You should be careful being so funny," I retorted with a straight face, "I think my sides have split. For your information I was looking at this."

I reached out and picked the letter up from the ground, where it had fallen. The paper felt old and brittle. It was nothing like the usual crisp white envelopes of my mysterious letters, but it had my name on the front in the same handwriting.

I tore open the envelope and read the letter with Zoe peering over my shoulder.

WHY DID THE ROMANS BUILD STRAIGHT ROADS?
SO THEIR SOLDIERS DIDN'T GO
ROUND THE BEND!

NEXT TIME YOU HAVE AN ADVENTURE, THERE'S
SOMETHING YOU NEED TO TAKE WITH YOU.

- I'M COLD AND I'M HARD, WITHOUT SINEW OR
  JOINT, BUT GIVE ME YOUR HAND AND I'LL MAKE
  A GOOD POINT.
- I WAS FORMED IN A FURNACE AND BEATEN TO BE.
  MY OWNER CAN USE ME TO KILL OR SET FREE.
- MUSTY AND DUSTY AND NOT FAR AWAY, THE
  PLACE WHERE I'M HIDING BEGINS WITH AN A.

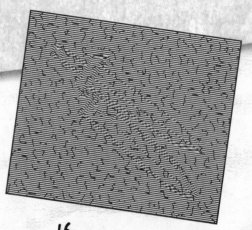

"I see the letters are still pretty cryptic," Zoe remarked. "Do you reckon the letter writer is trying to send you mental?"

I frowned. "Perhaps," I said, "but I'm finding these clues easier to understand."

"I'm glad someone is," she said in a dry tone.

"Think about it," I said, reading back over the clues. "It's something cold, hard and straight, with a point to it. It was made in a furnace – that's a fire – like a blacksmith or something. What does a blacksmith make?"

"Horseshoes?"

I rolled my eyes at her. "Yeah, like you can really set someone free or kill them with a horseshoe."

"Well, maybe if you whacked them over the head with it..."

She was grinning now, and I couldn't help but

Sometimes she says the dumbest things!!

grin back. We were on the trail of an Adventure at last! It felt great to be figuring out clues again.

"It's a sword!" I explained. "It's got to be. And as for where it's hidden..."

"I can get that!" Zoe exclaimed. "Somewhere dusty that begins with A – easy! It's the attic!"

"Then what are we waiting for?" I said excitedly. "Come on!"

Pausing only to deactivate the skateboard ramp and shove Morph into my pocket, we raced into the house, up the spiral staircase, past the bedrooms and up the stairs to the attic.

At the top Zoe leaned against the wall, panting, while I struggled to get the key out of my pocket. I found it in a secret hiding place not long after my parents went missing. Together with my amulet, it had led me to discover what it means to be a Solvit – and an Adventurer!

I fumbled as I pushed the key into the lock and turned it. The door swung open and I reached along the wall and turned on the dull orange light.

I peered at where she was pointing. Sure enough, concealed under a layer of dust, each sword had a small rectangle of cardboard next to it, with a description of the sword in old-fashioned handwriting. I used my thumb to clean the dust off the first label.

"Samurai sword, Japan, fourteenth century," I read aloud.

Zoe checked the next one. "Medieval sword, Britain, twelfth century," she said.

I liked the look of the next sword. It was very long and very thin, with an ornate, twisting hilt that looked as if it were made of gold. I was kind of disappointed when I found out that it was a rapier from the seventeenth century.

The next sword looked pretty ordinary in comparison. It was smaller and fairly short. Its hilt was wooden and looked knobbly.

"Gladius," I read from the label. "Rome, first century BC. Bingo!"

I lifted it carefully off the wall. The sword felt very real and powerful in my hand. It wasn't too heavy or too long – it might even fit in my backpack!

"Wow, it's amazing to think how old it is," said Zoe. "I wonder who it belonged to."

I peered at the shining blade.

"There's something engraved here," I said. "It's in Latin though – I can't read it."

Just as I said that, I felt the amulet around my neck grow warmer.

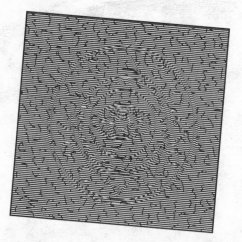

Then my eyes seemed to blur for a second, and when I looked at the engraving again, I could see that it said 'Titus'. I knew that the amulet worked as a translator for speech, but now it had started to work on writing as well!

A bubble of excitement rose up inside me. I had the sword, my amulet was working and the letter had told me that it was time to go. I couldn't wait to get started. Maybe this time I would find my mum!

"Let's go!" I cried.

But Zoe didn't move. She folded her arms across her chest and shook her head.

"Hang on, Time Boy."

"What's the matter?" I groaned. "I want to get to ancient Rome!"

"One," she said, "this attic is the single most awesome place I have ever seen and I want to explore it. Two: in case you've forgotten, Morph hasn't been exactly cooperative lately and you can't go anywhere unless Morph lets you."

She was holding up one hand and unfurling her

25

fingers as she made each point. I let out a long sigh and rolled my eyes at the ceiling.

"Three," she went on, "you should tell your grandpa where you're going. Four: you're not exactly dressed for ancient Rome. And five: you could at least wait until I've gone home before you start racing off in time. It's bad enough that I can't go with you."

Brain freeze – I had totally forgotten that Zoe's dad was visiting that weekend. I knew without asking that there was no way she could go off on an Adventure – she hardly ever gets to see him because he lives in Singapore. I could see the pleading look in her eyes.

"It's rubbish that you can't come," I said. "But Grandpa always says Adventures come first, and we can explore the attic any time. Now I've had that letter I'm positive that Morph will work as a time machine."

Zoe looked a bit sad but I knew she desperately wanted to see her dad.

"It's OK," she said, "I know you have to go. Come on, I'll help you get your Adventure tools together. I definitely want to come back and explore this place at some point though. My attic is nowhere near as amazing as this! Your grandpa must've been on some pretty cool Adventures."

We left the attic, with Zoe casting longing looks at all the amazing things it held. I locked the door and slipped the key back into my pocket. Then we raced down to my room – I had a lot to think about before setting off. On my last Adventure I had left my backpack behind and ended up in the Stone Age without so much as a bottle of truth serum. I wasn't going to let that happen again!

Ten minutes later I was standing in the middle of my room with my SurfM8 50 internet phone in my pocket and my backpack on my back. It was crammed with everything I thought I might need. I had packed:

- Camouflage paint
- Grandpa's spy diary
- Invisibility paint
- Steel rope
- Electric stun gun
- Supersonic screecher (designed to ward off dangerous animals)
- Super-strength fart gas (what was left of it)

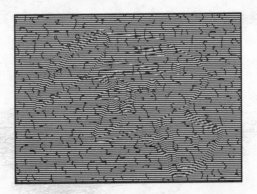

I was ready for action – all that remained was to put Morph to the test. Zoe crossed her fingers as I took a deep breath and activated Morph.

Success! The time machine stood in front of me and the door swung open – it was definitely Adventure time.

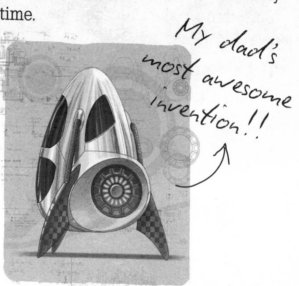

My dad's most awesome invention !!

"Good luck!" said Zoe, patting me on the back. "I hope you find your mum."

I grinned at her, feeling sorry that she couldn't come with me this time. I could see that she felt disappointed too.

"Will you let Grandpa know where I am?" I asked.

"Sure thing," she promised me. "Take care, Will."

"Don't worry about me," I said as I stepped inside Morph. "I'm prepared for anything!"

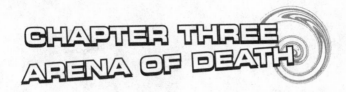
Stupidly, I stepped out of Morph without bothering to check where I was first. Remind me not to say 'I'm prepared for anything' ever again. I really should know better by now.

After the usual stomach-churning ride, Morph had landed in ancient Rome all right...slap-bang in the middle of a gladiator match! I quickly noticed three things:

- An unbelievably loud noise – the sound of thousands of people roaring and shrieking.
- A thin, bedraggled girl dressed in rags, cowering on the ground.
- A very angry-looking king of the beasts.

uh-oh!!

Yep, you guessed it. I was trapped in a massive arena with a terrified girl and a ravenous, furious lion. Thanks, Morph! I couldn't tell whether anyone had seen me arrive and at that moment I didn't really care. I 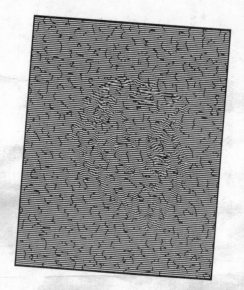 turned to leap back into Morph...and found only a miniature version of a time machine on the ground behind me.

"Dad designed you to shrink when you're not needed!" I bawled at the little object. "Get me out of here!"

Morph did nothing. I might as well have been

staring at a toy. But there was no time to lose – I had to get out of that arena fast! I shoved Morph into my backpack and swept a glance around me, trying to decide on the best thing to do.

The arena was made up of high stone benches around a sawdust circle. On one side of the circle was an oval archway with iron bars blocking it. There was another barred archway on the opposite side of the circle. Behind one archway stood five centurions with swords and shields. Behind the other archway prowled a second lion.

Iron bars + armed centurions + lions = No way out!

"Brilliant," I muttered.

My first thought was a mental vow to never again get out of Morph without looking. I just hoped that I'd have the chance to carry out that vow.

From the benches, thousands of people were cheering and yelling. They were obviously having a great time. It was as if they were at a football match or something. I have no idea how they thought they were civilized, because right at that moment they looked like barbarians to me!

My heart was thumping like fifteen drums and a brass band. A few metres away, the girl had her face pressed into the sawdust. She was shaking so hard that a little cloud of dust was rising around her. The lion was pacing around in front of her. It reminded me of a cat playing with a mouse. I felt as if I was frozen to the spot. I didn't know whether to be sick or scream or just drop to the ground like the girl.

Then a couple of things happened really fast.

First, the amulet suddenly grew super-hot and I could understand the chanting of the crowd – they were shouting 'Fight! Fight! Fight!'. Second, my legs started to work again, and before I could even think about it I was racing towards the lion!

I tugged my backpack open as I ran, and pulled out the first thing my hand touched. It was the supersonic screecher, and I pressed the button as hard as I could. Humans can't hear the sound it makes but animals can, and the lion went mental! It staggered sideways and then reared up, before running over to the barred archway and roaring in agony. The centurions on the other side of the bars backed away in fear.

There were shouts and gasps from the crowd. To them, it must have looked as if I just pointed at the lion and terrified it! Keeping my finger pressed down on the button, I leaned over the girl and dragged her to her feet.

"There's no time to explain!" I panted. "Just stay behind me and do exactly what I say!"

She nodded without making a sound – thankfully she wasn't the hysterical type. I turned to face the lion, dragging my backpack off. The lion was already getting used to the sound, and if it had been mad before, it was mad to the max now. It lolloped towards us, shaking its head to try and get rid of the noise.

I reached into my backpack and my hand closed around the super-strength fart gas. As the lion pounced at me, I squirted the gas right in its face. With a yowl of disgust, it tried to turn around in mid-air and fell in a golden heap on the ground in front of me.

The crowd went wild! If they had known my name they would have been chanting it. But at that moment I couldn't have cared less. The lion was hacking and coughing, but that had been the last squirt – the fart gas was all gone. I had used most of it to control my pet T-rex, and if I couldn't think of something else fast, this girl and I were officially stuffed.

I reached into my bag again, and this time I clutched at the cold steel rope.

I had to be quick! As soon as the lion got the smell out of its nostrils, it would be more determined than ever to eat me alive. Its massive claws were stained with what looked like blood, and I didn't fancy my chances against them. As the crowd screamed and cheered, I lifted one of the huge paws and tried to loop the rope around it.

"ROOOAAARRRRR!"

The lion flicked its paw and I did five somersaults backwards. My backpack flew off and its contents spilled out across the arena. The electric stun gun landed nearby, but already the ground was shaking as the lion thundered towards me. It was a powerhouse of muscle and sinew. There was no time to get up! I scrabbled across the sawdust-covered ground towards the stun gun. My fingers stretched out to pick it up...

"ROOOAAARRR!"

The lion launched itself at me, jaws gaping, as I grabbed the stun gun and pulled the trigger.

Waves of energy blasted towards the beast, like blue ripples in the air. The lion was knocked sideways and lay where it fell. It wasn't dead, but it would be out cold for hours.

The crowd erupted into applause, cheers and whistles. They thought I was some sort of super-gladiator or something! The girl looked white and shocked. She dropped to her knees and put her face in her hands. I guess that she had been expecting to die. She was still shaking, but I reckon this time it was in relief. All I wanted to do was collapse, but I couldn't risk anyone getting my Adventure tools. I stumbled across the sawdust to pick them up.

I was just zipping up my backpack when four guards stomped into the arena, their armour clinking. They dragged the girl to her feet and then grabbed me.

"You're coming with us," snarled one of the guards.

The girl clung to my arm, and I could feel her trembling. I was scared, but suddenly a wave of anger swept over me. We had just escaped death – what were they going to do with us now? Why couldn't they just leave us alone?

"Where are you taking us?" I shouted.

"Someone wants to see you," said the guard, leering into my face.

"Who?"

"Our lord and master!" he snarled, showing yellow teeth. "You're going to see Caesar!"

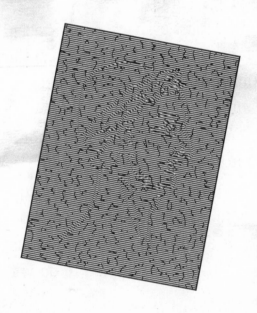

CHAPTER FOUR
CAESAR'S PALACE

"OK, I get the message!" I yelled.

The guards were pushing us through narrow streets, and if we slowed down for a second we were prodded in the back by sharp swords. I was getting angrier and angrier. Here I was in the glorious heart of the great Roman Empire, and I had no chance to take it all in. Thanks to Morph and a couple of thick-headed centurions, this was no time for sightseeing. Although actually, from what I saw of Rome I wasn't missing that much. I had expected clean, gleaming streets and breathtaking buildings, but it was all a bit dirty and cramped-looking.

I winced as I felt another dig in my back, and

looked at the girl who was being shoved along beside me.

"Thank you for saving me," she said in a low voice. "If I have to die, I would rather it were by sword than by lion."

"Why should you have to die?" I asked, feeling a bit queasy.

The girl shrugged as if it should be obvious.

"I am a slave," she said. "I was kidnapped from my homeland when the Romans conquered us and brought here to Rome. I was only two years old at the time so I don't remember much. But now, when the Romans get bored, they kill off a few slaves for entertainment. You must know what it's like? Well, today it's my turn."

"Er, in case you hadn't noticed, I'm not exactly from around here," I said. "I thought the Roman Empire was meant to be civilized? This is crazy!"

"It's civilized for the citizens," the girl whispered. "But slaves and gladiators aren't citizens – we're nothing."

She sounded resigned, but when I looked into her big brown eyes, I saw a flicker of wildness. She reminded me a bit of Zoe. I reckoned that all the years of slavery had worn her down, but they hadn't quite got rid of her spark.

"My name's Will," I said. "And you're not nothing."

"I'm Eleni," she replied with a sudden smile. "Thank you for saving my life, Will."

"Shut up, slave scum!" bellowed the guard, jabbing me with his sword again.

I was beginning to worry about meeting Julius Caesar. Why did he want to see us?

Half an hour later we were standing in the middle of a vast hall. We had been pushed, prodded and kicked, and now we were in serious trouble. But I almost forgot about the danger when I saw how rich Caesar was.

The hall was lined with massive statues that made the ones at Solvit Hall look like small chess pieces. The ceiling was so high that I had to screw up my eyes to see the paintings on them. Thick marble pillars were positioned around the room, and rich tapestries and velvets hung on the walls. The floor was made of polished marble, inlaid with gold. It was totally, totally awesome.

The hall was swarming with people. Apart from the guards behind us, there were tons of stern-looking centurions and soldiers. They all looked deadly serious. There were guys in togas, slaves scurrying around in plain white tunics and women wandering around in long, floaty dresses. They all looked down their noses at Eleni, and stared at me as if I was from outer space. I guess they weren't used to jeans and T-shirts in ancient Rome.

Suddenly all the scurrying doubled in speed and there was a whooshing sound as if fifty people had sucked in their breath at the same time. I felt a heavy hand on my shoulder and I was forced onto my knees. The same hand pressed on the back of my neck until my nose nearly touched the cold floor. Out of the corner of my eye I could see that the same thing had happened to Eleni.

A deep voice shouted, "Hail Caesar!" and then everyone joined in, chanting the words over and over again, getting louder and louder. I heard a thump to my left and saw that one of the women had fainted with excitement.

"So, this is the slave who defeated the lion?" asked a strong, deep voice. "He does not look like a slave to me. Arise, boy."

I stood up and saw a tall man standing in front of me. He had curly brown hair and was wearing a cream toga. There was something about the crinkles around his eyes that made me think this guy had a sense of humour. I relaxed a bit. If he was as intelligent as he looked, maybe I was going to be OK.

"Er, Hail Caesar," I said.

I thought that the guy's eyes were going to pop out of his head!

"Do you not know your own lord and master?" he cried. "I am not Caesar!"

There was a high-pitched, annoyed squeak, and then a short, plump man stepped out in front of me. He was draped in a purple toga and his

Ooops!! Big mistake!

mouth was turned down at the corners.

"I am Caesar!" he declared in a sulky, shrill voice.

My heart sank. He looked about as friendly as the lion – but not quite as clever. Caesar settled himself into a plush velvet chair and waggled his fat fingers at the man beside him.

"Question him!" he demanded.

The tall man had not taken his eyes off me.

"I am Mark Antony," he said.

"I'm Will," I said.

"Will, how is it that you do not recognize the man whose face is on every coin?"

I could feel danger in the air around me. It was like static electricity, and it made the hairs on my arms and on the back of my neck rise up. I gave a little shiver.

"I'm not from around here," I said. "I just...er... arrived."

"Yes, right in the middle of the arena, so I understand," said Mark Antony with a hint of a smile.

I didn't reply because I was staring at Caesar. He had pulled out a small hand mirror and was gazing at his own reflection, pushing stray strands of hair into place. He caught me looking at him and wrinkled up his nose as if he could smell a fart.

"Is this witchcraft, Mark Antony?" he asked in that high, quavering voice. "I was told he appeared as if by magic."

"I'm not a wizard!" I declared.

"Then you won't object if I look inside your strange bag?" Mark Antony asked.

Before I could reply, one of the guards had wrenched my backpack off. He threw it to Mark Antony, who opened it and peered inside. I was expecting him to look surprised or to ask about my tools. But his expression didn't change at all.

Mark Antony pulled out the sword I had found in Grandpa's attic. He looked at it closely, and then gazed into my eyes. There was no hint of

a smile now. I thought about all the battles this
guy fought and won in his lifetime. Mark Antony
was a born soldier. He had something about him
that meant you didn't want to take your eyes off
him...and you definitely didn't want him to be
looking at you like that.

"I recognize this sword," he said. "It belongs to
Titus Solvit."

His voice was quiet, but the power behind it
made me shiver.

"Our missing general!" Caesar gasped. "What
does this mean?"

"One thing is certain," said Mark Antony. "Will
is not from any land I have ever known."

My thoughts whizzed around my head. Titus
Solvit must be one of my ancestors. Maybe this
Adventure had nothing to do with finding my
parents at all – maybe I had to find Titus! While

I was thinking, Caesar had stood up and shoved Mark Antony aside. His puffy face was pale. He pointed at me with a shaking finger.

"It is a clear sign!" Caesar declared. "This boy is a gift from the gods!"

I hope this is a good thing

"Hold it right there!" I said.

There was a horrified gasp from the people in the hall, but I didn't care. Last time I was declared to be a gift from a god I was nearly sacrificed, and I didn't fancy going through that again. Mark Antony was frowning, and for a second I thought he had a sort of warning in his eyes. But all I could focus on was saving myself from being another sacrifice to another god.

"Let's get one thing straight," I said, looking Caesar straight in the eye. "I am not a gift from any god."

I thought Caesar's eyes were going to pop out of his head. His face turned first red and then purple.

"No one argues with Caesar!" he screeched. "Apologize, scum!"

"I'm not saying sorry for telling the truth," I retorted. "And I'm not scum!"

I think Caesar forgot how to speak for a moment. His mouth opened and closed like a goldfish. Mark Antony closed his eyes, and I heard Eleni whimper beside me.

"Arguing with Caesar is a crime," Caesar hissed at last, "and you and your friend will pay for it. You may have beaten a lion, but you won't find Vilius and Livius so easy to defeat!"

Eleni gave a little moan.

"Who are Vilius and Livius?" I asked her.

"They're the biggest, strongest gladiators in the whole of the Empire!" she said, her voice shaking. "They're the best. Nobody fights them and comes out alive."

Great. We were going back into the arena.

Half an hour later Eleni and I were standing behind one of the gates to the arena. My legs had started to feel like overcooked spaghetti. Mark Antony still had my backpack, and without Morph and my Adventure kit I was 100% stuffed. There was only one good thing about the situation: it definitely couldn't get any worse.

I peered through the bars of the gate. Vilius and Livius had been busy. The arena was littered with torn-off limbs and spattered with blood. The two gladiators were chopping up their latest victim, and the crowd was waving at them and chanting their names. I could even see a few banners

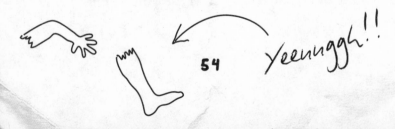

saying things like 'Marry Me, Vilius!' and 'We Love Livius!'. It was the Roman version of a reality TV show.

The thought of what was about to happen had sent me into a state of silent shock, but as I looked at the spectators howling for blood, I had a thought that kick-started my Adventuring skills. Somewhere in that crowd, Caesar was taking his place, preparing to get his revenge on me. My fear evaporated in a rush of anger.

"How vain and spoiled do you have to be to have someone killed for arguing with you?" I seethed to Eleni. "Who does he think he is?"

"The leader of the known world with absolute power over life and death," she replied in a dull, hopeless voice.

Suddenly the guards behind us parted, and Mark Antony appeared. He put his hand on my shoulder and got straight to the point.

"I have no wish to see you die," he said. "There is something...special about you. I have petitioned for you. Caesar has agreed that if you can win this match, he will set you both free. If not..."

His eyes strayed towards a ripped and bloody forearm lying in the sawdust, and my stomach sank into my shoes.

"How are we supposed to defeat the two best gladiators in Rome?" I asked.

"I have a feeling that this might help," Mark Antony said.

He pulled my backpack from underneath his toga!

"Awesome!" I cried, hugging it to my chest. "Thank you!"

He wished us luck, turned on his heel and

strode away. Let me tell you right now – if you look up 'cool' in the dictionary, you'll see a picture of Mark Antony.

The crowd quietened and the guards swung the barred gates open. It was time to stare death in the face for the second time that day. Eleni and I looked at each other and sighed.

"Can you do two miracles in one day?" she asked shakily.

"I don't know," I said, taking a deep and slightly shaky breath. "But I'll give it a go."

Then we were pushed forwards and the gate clanged shut behind us. This was it – there was no escape.

"Vilius and Livius versus Will and Eleni!" boomed a voice.

"VILIUS! VILIUS! VILIUS!" chanted the crowd. "LIVIUS! LIVIUS! LIVIUS!"

Vilius and Livius were gigantic, armed and deadly, but we had one major advantage over them. We were small. The two men were muscle-bound and weighed down by heavy golden armour, but we could move like lightning.

I fumbled in my backpack, grabbed the steel rope and passed one end of it to Eleni.

"Hold on to that and don't let go," I said quietly. "Now, you're going to run around the arena one way, and I'm going to run the other way. Ready?"

Eleni nodded, her eyes wide.

"GO!" I yelled.

We sprinted away from each other, drawing the steel rope tight and then whipping it hard against the gladiators. Before they could duck or run, Eleni and I had passed each other and the steel rope caught the two men in a hard circle.

Around and around we ran, with the gladiators looking more and more confused. They growled at us in disbelief as they realised they were trapped. Within seconds their arms were pinned to their sides, their weapons useless.

"Stop!" Vilius bellowed, looking like an enraged bull. "I'll tear out your liver! I'll rip off your arms and make you eat them!"

"Tempting, but no thanks!" I called back.

Eleni and I kept circling the gladiators, winding the steel rope around their chests and legs, until all that could be seen of them were their infuriated expressions.

We finished with a double knot, and then I stood beside them and gave them a tiny push. They wobbled for a moment, and then fell to the floor with a sickening THUMP, sending sawdust up around them in clouds.

There was a moment of utter silence in the arena, and then a rumbling cheer arose. Among the roars and whistles, I could hear a chant: "WILL! WILL! WILL! ELENI! ELENI! ELENI!"

I grinned at Eleni and she grinned right back. We had won!

CHAPTER SIX
A CLUE AT LAST

The crowd poured into the arena and we were
patted, hugged and kissed. Hundreds of voices
clamoured for our autographs, begged us to pose
for sketches and screamed our names. In the
space of ten minutes we had gone from zeros to
heroes...and I was hating it. I caught Eleni's eye
and she jerked her head towards the gate.

"Want to get out of here?" she asked.

She dropped to the ground and I followed
her. We scurried away on our hands and knees,
weaving through legs until we reached the gate.
It was standing open with no guards to block our
way. We crawled inside the long corridor that
led to the main exit. It was dark and a bit smelly,

but at the moment it was the coolest place in the world!

"I can't believe it!" said Eleni as we jumped to our feet. "I'm free!"

"That's brilliant," I said. "What are you going to – WOW!"

I pounced on the white envelope that was lying on the ground in front of us. It was another letter!

WHY DID JULIUS CAESAR BUY CRAYONS?
HE WANTED TO MARK ANTONY!

YOU DID AN AWESOME JOB IN THE ARENA, WILL, BUT YOU CAN'T STOP BATTLING JUST YET. YOU MUST FIND TITUS!

GO TO THE PLACE WHERE CASTOR AND POLLUX APPEARED. STAND UPON THEIR FACES.

THE ANSWER IS IN JUPITER'S HAND.

WILL'S FACT FILE

Dear Adventurer,

I expect you already know a lot about the ancient Romans. But did you know that they spoke Latin? And have you heard of Romulus and Remus? They were twin brothers who were abandoned at birth and raised by a wolf. When they grew up, Romulus founded Rome after killing his brother in a quarrel. Poor Remus!

This fact file is packed with lots of cool stuff about Rome and the Romans. Check out the facts and timeline and amaze your mates with your knowledge.

TIMELINE

753 BC
According to legend, Rome is founded by Romulus.

753–510 BC
Rome is ruled by kings.

510 BC
Republic of Rome begins when the citizens vote for two ruling consuls.

54 BC
Julius Caesar again invades Britain but then leaves it in peace for 100 years.

55 BC
Julius Caesar leads the first unsuccessful invasion of Britain.

218 BC
Hannibal of Carthage is defeated when he invades Rome.

45 BC
Julius Caesar gets an Egyptian astronomer to create a new 12-month calendar.

44 BC
Julius Caesar is assassinated.

49–45 BC
Julius Caesar leads and wins a Civil War and becomes ruler.

27 BC
Julius Caesar's nephew, Augustus, declares himself emperor and the Roman Empire begins.

50 AD
The Romans found Londinium in England.

43 AD
The invasion of Britain begins.

61 AD
Boudicca leads a rebellion against the Roman invaders in Britain.

122–130 AD
The Romans build Hadrian's Wall.

410 AD
The Romans lose control of Britain.

455 AD
Rome is destroyed by barbarians and the Empire is no more.

JULIUS CAESAR

Who was he?
He was a brilliant Roman general and statesman.

When was he born?
100 BC.

Why was he so important?
In 49 BC he seized power and became the ruler of Rome.

What was his title?
Dictator.

Who was his girlfriend?
Cleopatra, Queen of Egypt.

What did he dislike?
He hated being a baldy and tried to hide his bald patch by combing his hair forward!

Did he have any major weaknesses?
He suffered from epilepsy.

When did he die?
Julius Caesar was stabbed to death by assassins on March 15 (Ides of March), 44 BC.

Why was he killed?
Because he wanted to become King.

Who killed Julius Caesar?
Brutus and other members of the Senate.

Did you know?
Before Julius Caesar gave us the modern 12-month calendar, there were only 10 months in the year.

Roman rulers
- Rome used to be ruled by kings.
- Tarquin the Proud was the last king.
- Tarquin was such a tyrant that he was overthrown and Rome became a republic.
- The republic lasted for 450 years, until Augustus became the first emperor.

Did you know? A republic is a country without a king or emperor.

Society
- Roman people were either citizens or non-citizens.
- Citizens were divided into 3 classes: patricians (nobles), equites (knights) and plebeians (ordinary workers).
- Non-citizens included women, slaves and foreigners.

Did you know? Rome was governed by a group of powerful men, known as the Senate.

Children
- Babies were given a bulla (a sort of lucky charm) to wear.
- Only wealthy boys went to school.
- When a boy was about 15 he burnt his toys and put on a toga!
- Girls could get married when they were just 12 years old.

Did you know? When a baby was born, his father could decide whether or not it would live.

Slaves

- Slaves did most of the hard and dirty work in ancient Rome.
- Slaves had no rights and could be beaten, or killed, by their owner.
- All slaves had to wear identity tags.
- Roman citizens could be forced into slavery if they couldn't pay debts.

Did you know? If a Roman father didn't like his child, he could sell it into slavery!

Harsh treatment

- Non-citizens who committed crimes could be punished by being nailed to a cross and left to die (crucified).
- Citizens could be banished from Rome.
- In ancient Egypt, they used trained dogs and monkeys to help enforce the law! But in ancient Rome, they used the army.

Did you know? If you said anything bad about the emperor, you could have your tongue cut out.

Strange ideas

- The Ancient Romans had many strange ideas and superstitions.
- They had a god or goddess for everything from love (Venus) to partying (Bacchus).
- They predicted the future by studying animal guts.

Did you know? Seeing a woman carrying a spindle was bad luck.

The Roman army

- The Roman army was made up of foot soldiers, called legionaries, and leaders called centurions.
- The army was divided into units, called centuries. These were organized into bigger groups called legions.

Did you know? Centurions carried sticks to beat disobedient soldiers.

Soldier's life

- Legionaries had to sign up for 25 years and couldn't marry.
- They had to march for up to 20 Roman miles in a day carrying weapons, food and sleeping gear.
- Part of a soldier's wage was a salt allowance called a salarium.

Did you know? The English word for salary (meaning wages) comes from the Latin word 'salarium'.

Enemies of Rome

- Hannibal of Carthage (in North Africa) terrified the Romans with his army of war elephants.
- The Celts were a ferocious bunch, who went into battle naked and collected their enemies' heads as trophies.

Did you know? Romans called foreigners 'barbarians' because they thought their speech sounded like a sheep's 'baa'.

Great builders and engineers

- The Romans are famous for their straight, paved roads.
- Their plumbing was very advanced, with aqueducts, public fountains, toilets and heated baths.
- They built colossal amphitheatres, like the Colosseum that could seat 50,000 people.

Did you know? The Romans invented cement!

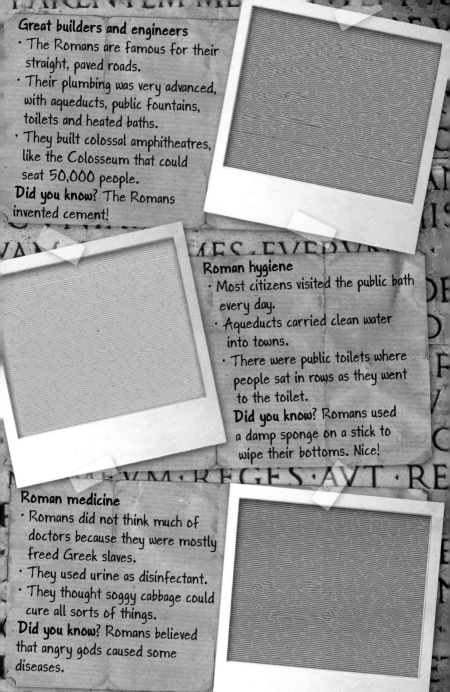

Roman hygiene

- Most citizens visited the public bath every day.
- Aqueducts carried clean water into towns.
- There were public toilets where people sat in rows as they went to the toilet.

Did you know? Romans used a damp sponge on a stick to wipe their bottoms. Nice!

Roman medicine

- Romans did not think much of doctors because they were mostly freed Greek slaves.
- They used urine as disinfectant.
- They thought soggy cabbage could cure all sorts of things.

Did you know? Romans believed that angry gods caused some diseases.

Food and feasts

- Most Romans ate simple meals of bread, beans and wheat.
- Rich hosts served camels' feet and ostrich brains to their guests.
- Guests ate until they were sick. Then they'd go back for more!

Did you know? There were no tomatoes or pasta in ancient Rome, and definitely no pizza!

Fun and games

- Chariot racing was the most popular form of entertainment, closely followed by gladiator fights.
- Charioteers regularly fell off.
- Chariot racing took place on a giant circuit in Rome.

Did you know? Chariot racing was taken so seriously that sometimes fights broke out between rival fans.

Gladiator games

- At gladiator games people watched men and animals fight to the death.
- Gladiators were normally slaves or criminals.
- The arena floor was covered in sand to soak up the blood.

Did you know? Successful gladiators were the pop stars of their day.

Where was his hand??

"Just when I thought I was starting to get the hang of these," I groaned.

"What is it?" Eleni asked.

After all we'd been through, I decided to trust her. I explained everything to her as quickly and simply as I could. I told her about time travel and about being from the future. I told her about my mysterious letters and about my search to find my parents. She took it amazingly well.

"You must have seen some wonderful things," she said in a soft voice.

"You're not freaked out?" I asked.

Eleni shrugged. "I have been stolen from my people and lived so long as a slave that I have forgotten who I am," she said. "I have faced death in the arena. I have wallowed in the gutters of Rome and I have stood in front of Caesar. Right now, I think anything is possible."

"You reckon?" I replied. "I'd say solving these clues is pretty impossible."

Eleni looked at them and shrugged her shoulders.

"I don't understand the language," she said.

Of course! The letter was written in English – the only reason I could speak to Eleni was because the amulet was translating for me. I read the clues aloud, and Eleni smiled.

"The first clue is easy," she said. "Rome is teeming with

stories about the gods."

"Castor and Pollux are gods?" I asked.

"They're the twin sons of Jupiter," she said,
nodding.

"Jupiter – I know about him!" I said. "He's top
god, isn't he?"

Eleni nodded again. "Castor and Pollux once
helped the Romans win a difficult battle. Then
they appeared in the city to announce victory. To
celebrate, the Romans built a temple on the spot
where they appeared."

"That must be it!" I cried. "Do you know where
it is?"

"Of course – it's right in the heart of the city,"
she told me. "Come on, I'll show you the way."

She grabbed my arm and together we ran away
from the stadium.

Twenty minutes later I was looking at the Temple of Castor and Pollux, and for a moment I couldn't speak. The temple would have taken my breath away if I weren't already puffed out from all the running. Among all the dirty, crumbling buildings of the narrow streets, the temple was a sort of mini miracle.

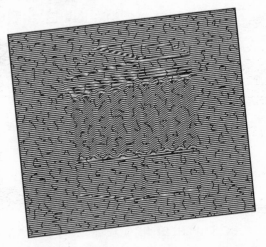

It was made of white stone that gleamed in the afternoon sun. Eight vast columns marked the entrance. It looked as if it had been built by giants. Marble steps led up to an ornate doorway, and a whole bunch of snooty-looking guys in togas were streaming out of it. They walked two by two, talking in low voices.

"They are the Senators," said Eleni.

I scrabbled for the letter in my pocket and smoothed it out.

"It says we have to stand on the faces of Castor and Pollux," I said. "How are we supposed to stand on the faces of imaginary gods?"

"What are you saying?" said Eleni, looking horrified. "The gods have struck people down for comments like that!"

I was about to argue when I realized that there was a time and a place for religious debate, and this wasn't it. Right now I had a temple to explore and an ancient Solvit ancestor to locate.

"Well, does the clue mean anything to you?" I asked.

"I think it must mean something inside the temple," Eleni replied. "There's an inner chamber where the Senators meet."

"So what are we waiting for?" I asked. "Let's get in there!"

No one gave us a second glance as we ran up the steps and slipped inside the temple. A long, empty chamber stretched out in front of us. Eleni hesitated, but I raced inside and looked at the floor.

"Brilliant!" I cried.

A huge mosaic covered almost the whole floor. It showed two shining warriors on horseback, looking up at the sky.

"Castor and Pollux, right?" I asked Eleni. "Hey, what's wrong?"

She had gone really pale.

"It's just...we shouldn't be in here," she said in a rush. "The Senators will have us arrested if they find us."

"We'd better hurry up then, hadn't we?" I said with a grin.

I stood on the mosaic face of Castor, and Eleni stood on Pollux. I stared around me, trying to figure out what the last clue meant. The answer is in Jupiter's hand.

"Look!" Eleni exclaimed. "Jupiter!"

She pointed at the top of the mosaic. Among the painted clouds, I could see a man with a long white beard. We hadn't been able to see him before, because he was formed from what looked like random bits of cloud. But when we stood on the faces, the angle was just right and all the pieces fitted together. ←

So cool!

71

"It's a trick picture!" I said.

We ran over to the mosaics that formed his hand, but the hand was empty. I frowned – the letters had lied to me! Then the explanation flashed into my mind.

"It's not in his hand, it's under it!" I exclaimed. "Under the mosaic tiles!"

Perhaps Titus was being held captive in an underground prison or something! I knelt down and levered one of the mosaics up. But instead of earth or a trapdoor beneath it, I saw a bit of white paper. Eleni gasped and kneeled down to help me.

It only took a few seconds to force up the rest of the mosaics, and then I was holding another letter in my hand! For once there was no joke and no cryptic clue – just five simple words:

TITUS IS IN ELENI'S HOMELAND.

When I read the letter aloud, Eleni's mouth fell open.

"How can I be mentioned in your letter?" she asked. "We've only just met!"

"I don't know," I told her. "I've given up trying to understand how the letters know so much. What's your homeland?"

"Gaul," she said.

I groaned. Gaul was the ancient name for France and we were in Italy. We had a looooong journey ahead.

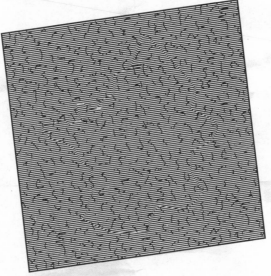

Eleni's eyes were shining.

"Will, I'm coming with you," she said. "I'm going home!"

There was no time to lose. We had to get to

Gaul as fast as we could, and it was hundreds of miles away. Without maps or transport, we would have to rely on luck to get us there in one piece.

Eleni led me through the streets until we reached the city boundaries. A vast city gate was the only thing that stood between us and Adventure. But as we ran towards it, a loud cry went up behind us, and the words made my heart sink.

"Halt in the name of Caesar! You're both under arrest!"

History was repeating itself way too soon for my liking. Once again we were kneeling in front of Caesar with a hall full of people gawping at us. Once again Mark Antony was watching us with a grave expression. I just hoped our next stop wouldn't be the arena.

"I thought you said Caesar would set us free if we won," I said to Mark Antony.

"Indeed," Mark Antony replied. "But I didn't know you would race off before we had time to speak to you."

I felt a little prickle of danger, and made up my mind to make a run for it if they mentioned putting me back in the arena.

Noooo way!!!

"I wished to congratulate you," said Caesar. "You are a fine warrior. You may kiss my hand."

"Oh good, thanks," I muttered, sceptically raising an eyebrow.

He held out his pale, chubby hand. It looked clammy and limp, and I could see the rings digging into the puffy flesh. It made me feel a bit sick.

I was wondering how to get out of this one when Eleni darted forward and kissed it. Thankfully Caesar seemed satisfied with that, coz there was no way I was kissing his hand. I'd rather have walked back into that arena and kissed the lion.

"Tell me," said Caesar, settling into his throne and rearranging his toga. "Where were you hurrying off to so fast?"

I could see no point in lying to him.

"I'm going to Gaul to search for Titus Solvit,"
I said.

Curiosity flashed into Mark Antony's intelligent brown eyes, but Caesar just stifled a yawn with the back of his hand.

"Fascinating," he mumbled.

Mark Antony leaned towards him and murmured something.

"Yes, yes, very well," said Caesar. "Young man, I am sending Mark Antony and a few legions to Gaul, to check that all is well there. As you and your friend are heading that way, you can travel with the army."

I had been so ready to hear that I'd be facing another gladiator, it took a few seconds for my brain to register what Caesar had said. Travelling with the army? That was great news! We'd get there much faster and they'd protect us along the way too.

"Wow!" I said. "Thank you!"

I hadn't been looking forward to trying to find my way to France. Mark Antony nodded his head at me, and I guessed that this was his doing.

"Tonight there is a farewell feast to prepare for the journey ahead," Caesar said, licking his lips and clasping his hands over his stomach. "You will be the guests of honour."

I thanked him again, but my heart wasn't really in it. I was pretty sure that Caesar changed his mood as often as he changed his toga. Right now I was a favourite; tomorrow I could be thrown to the lions. The sooner I was out of Rome, the better. In the meantime, a Roman banquet sounded like a fantastic idea.

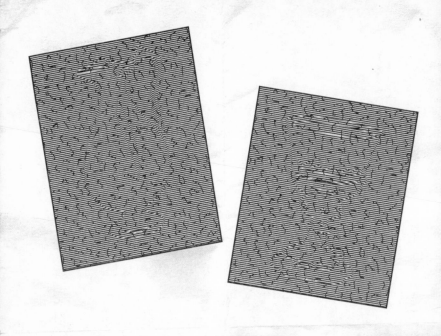

Whatever I've said against Caesar, I'll say this: the guy knew how to throw a party!

The feast was held in another, grander hall of Caesar's palace. The moment Eleni and I walked in, two servant girls brought us perfumed water to wash our hands and feet. I didn't really want to stink of perfume, but everyone else was doing it and I didn't want to give Caesar a reason to be mad with me.

Next, the girls led us towards the feasting area. Three massive couches were arranged in a U-shape around a long, low table. Each couch was made to fit nine people! I was seated with Caesar on my right and Eleni on my left, and Mark Antony was on Caesar's other side. I kept my eye on him, since I had no idea what I was supposed to do. Eleni looked even more nervous than I felt. She was used to waiting on Romans, not dining with them.

The whole thing began with a sort of prayer to Jupiter, and then everyone leaned on the couches, so I did the same. A golden plate was pressed into my left hand, and a golden goblet stood on the table in front of me. The plate felt heavy and warm. Then an army of servants in white tunics brought silver platters of food to the table.

There were plates of small boiled birds, an entire roast goat and snails fed with milk.

A group of servants sang to us. They were amazing!

My goblet was filled with horrible wine that was as thick as treacle.

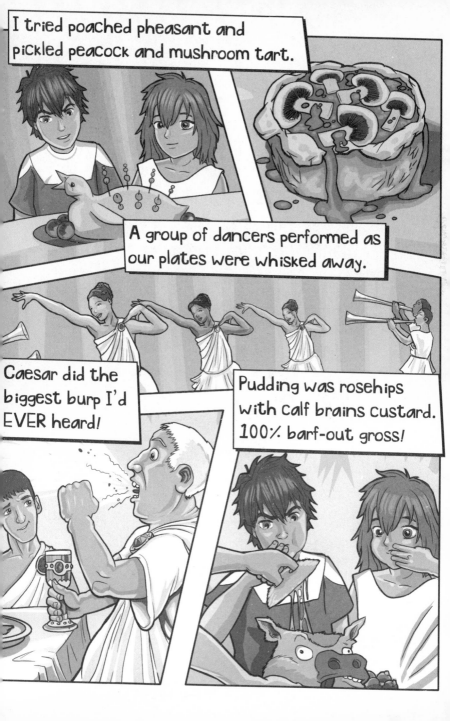

The last course was accompanied by a group of acrobats in bright costumes. They cartwheeled and back-flipped around us as we ate. They stood on each others' shoulders, and basically did just about everything except swing from the ceiling. It was incredible. I couldn't take my eyes off them, but the other guests seemed to take it for granted.

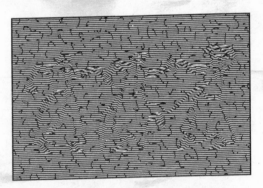

I had gone past the point of being able to speak by this point, and my vision had gone a bit blurry. (Also I was trying to not think about the calf brains custard.) Eleni had fallen asleep with her

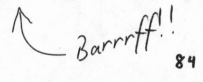

Barrrff!!

head on the table, and my stomach was making some very weird noises. It was definitely time for bed.

As I drifted off to sleep under silken covers, reeking of perfume, I wondered what was going to happen to me next. It had been a pretty eventful day, and I had a feeling that things were only going to get weirder. In the morning we would be setting off for Gaul with Mark Antony and three Roman legions. The next stage of my Adventure was about to begin.

"Relax! Balance! Cut! Sidestep! Bend your elbows! Parry!"

I tried to obey all Mark Antony's instructions at once, tripped over a grassy tuft and fell flat on my face. Mark Antony stood over me with his arms folded, laughing merrily.

"Very funny," I groaned, pulling myself to my feet and rubbing my knee.

"Not so funny if you had been in a real sword fight," he said. "You'd be dead with a sword in your back. You must always keep one eye on the terrain."

"One eye on the opponent, one eye on the ground, one eye on the battle," said Eleni, who

Totally cool guy

was watching from a distance. "How many eyes do you think he's got?"

I was getting pretty good at sword fighting by now, but I was still making stupid mistakes, and I knew that they could cost me more than a sore knee. I was determined to keep trying, though. Sword fighting was a skill that could come in handy on future Adventures

– plus, being able to sword fight was mega cool.

We had been travelling for months, and it had been a hard slog, but I had enjoyed every minute so far. Apart from the occasional fight with barbarians, it had been a steady round of marching, sleeping, eating and sword fighting. I had no idea of the date, but I was pretty sure I must have turned eleven by now. Eleni was bored sick of it, but she was eager to get home. I was just enjoying being taught battle skills by one of the greatest generals in history.

At first I had been worried about being away from home for so long. I had tried – and failed – to get Morph to transform into a time machine. The message was clear – I was stuck here. Morph wouldn't turn into anything at all, and in the end I decided not to worry about it any more. Mark Antony's calm attitude was rubbing off on me. He was awesome. His soldiers loved him because he was always fair, as well as being decisive and brave and all the other things they wanted their generals to be.

That night, after we had set up camp and eaten, Eleni and I relaxed in Mark Antony's tent.

"How far are we from Gaul now?" Eleni asked.

"You've asked that question every night for a month," said Mark Antony. "Can't you be patient, Eleni?"

She went red, and I felt sorry for her.

"Imagine how she's feeling," I said to Mark Antony. "She hasn't seen her parents for years – not since she was a little girl. Something like that never goes out of your mind."

I felt really sad as I thought about my own mum and dad, separated from each other and me, somewhere in time and space. I had never

I know exactly how she feels

told Mark Antony anything about them or where I came from, and he had never asked. But I could see a familiar, curious gleam in his eyes.

"Have you ever seen this woman?" I asked on impulse.

I pulled a photo of my mum out of my pocket and handed it to him. His eyes widened.

"What magic is this?" he asked. "I have never seen an image like it. It's as if she is standing in front of me!"

Oops. I forgot that photos weren't exactly common in ancient Rome. And I couldn't explain anything to him. You see, I felt as if telling Eleni was OK. After all, she wasn't going to turn out to be a great figure in history or anything. Who'd listen to a poor ex-slave? But Mark Antony was going to end up ruling a third of the world. If he knew about time travel, history could start getting a bit crazy.

Luckily, he seemed to have a sixth sense about things like that.

"Say nothing, Will," he said. "I can see that you cannot speak to me of this. But it is...a wonderful thing."

"Thanks," I muttered, feeling a bit awkward. He had taught me so much and shared his skills and knowledge with me. I hoped he didn't think that I didn't trust him or something.

"She looks like you," he said. "Is she your mother?"

I nodded and he gave a sad smile.

"I'm sorry, Will, I have never seen her," he said.

I took the photo back and stood up.

"I'm just going to get some air," I said.

I stepped out of the tent and took a deep breath.

I hadn't really thought Mum could be here. It was pretty obvious that this Adventure was all about Titus. But suddenly a great big wave of missing her had crashed over me, and I didn't feel like talking any more.

I strolled towards my tent, kicking at the dark grass. All around me were the sounds of the soldiers – eating, singing and talking. Lights glimmered in the darkness like stars. There was an icy chill in the air.

I found myself wondering what sort of sky my parents were looking up at. Maybe Mum was even looking at the same stars as me, but I was pretty sure that Dad was somewhere I couldn't even imagine.

According to the most recent clue, Dad had disappeared off in a spaceship with a bunch of aliens called the Partek. For all I knew, he could be on another planet at that moment, looking at the Earth and wondering about me.

As I reached my tent, the moon came out from behind a cloud and illuminated our camping ground.

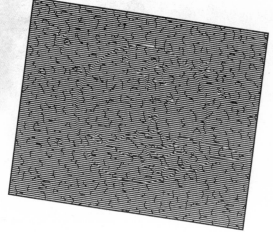

In the sudden silver gleam, I saw something that made my heart start to hammer against my ribs as if it wanted to get out. There was a letter pinned to the tent flap!

My hands were shaking as I tore the envelope open and tugged the sheet of paper out.

OLD KINGS NEVER DIE.
THEY JUST GET THRONE AWAY!

WILL, THIS IS YOUR BIGGEST ADVENTURE YET.
YOU DON'T HAVE MUCH LONGER TO WAIT. YOU WILL
FIND TITUS WHEN YOU FIND THE KING OF GAUL.
THEIR HIDING PLACE IS EVERYONE'S GRAVE.
NO MINOTAUR WAITS HERE, BUT EVERY TREASURE
NEEDS A PROTECTOR.

My mood changed instantly. I went from miserable to happy faster than a speeding Ferrari.

Then I heard a soft sound behind me and saw Eleni hurrying towards me.

"Will, are you OK?" she asked.

"I am now!" I said, almost yelling the words in my excitement. "Check this out."

I read the letter to her and her brow furrowed.

"What does it mean?" she asked. "What is 'everyone's grave'?"

Of course, when she asked the question like that, the answer was obvious.

"The earth!" I shouted. "They must be underground!"

Eleni clutched my arm in excitement.

"Will, it's a labyrinth!" she cried. "A massive underground maze! I heard the story of the minotaur when I was a slave – it was a beast that was trapped in a labyrinth!"

I held my hand up for Eleni to high-five me, but

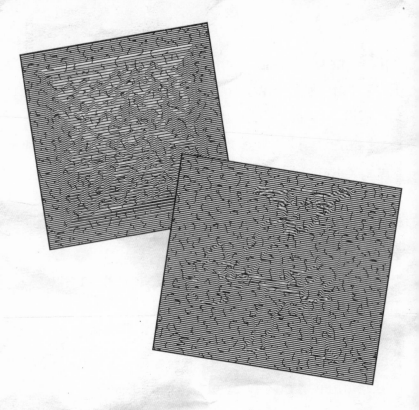

she didn't get it.

"Never mind," I said, lowering my hand. "Eleni, you're brilliant," I told her. "I would never have been able to guess that!"

"There's something else about the letter," Eleni

continued. "I feel as if there's something I should recognize or remember."

I felt a rush of exhilaration. Soon I'd meet Titus, a great general and my Roman ancestor. And finally I'd find out what this Adventure was really all about!

CHAPTER NINE
THE KING OF GAUL

After months and months of travelling, we finally
arrived in Gaul and marched into a city called
Avaricum. It felt amazing to be a part of the
Roman army. As we headed towards the castle
at the centre of the city, people came out of their
houses and lined the streets to watch us pass.
I saw the soldiers puffing out their chests with
pride as we marched. They knew how cool they
looked!

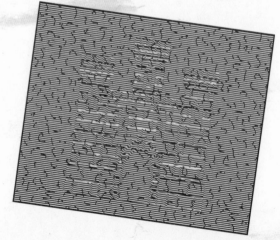

"How does it feel to be home?" I asked Eleni as we arrived at the castle.

"Strange," she said after a pause. "It's like trying to remember a dream. There are so many things that I've forgotten, but I know they're still in my memory – I just need to find them."

She had a far-away look in her eyes. I could guess that she was thinking about her parents – because that's exactly what I would have been doing.

We were greeted by a whole load of important-looking people, but I could see that Mark Antony was looking confused. He approached a scared-looking man.

"What's your name, man?" he asked abruptly.

"Qu-Qu-Quentin, my lord," the man replied.

"Quentin, I demand you to tell me where the King is," Mark Antony ordered.

"I...c-c-can't say, my lord!" stammered the man. "I...er...was sworn to secrecy – on pain of death!"

"Death will find you very soon if you don't answer my questions," said Mark Antony, his hand on his sword.

Quentin was shaking so much that he could hardly stand up. I felt sorry for him, and I had an idea. I stepped forward. Mark Antony gave me a surprised look, but waved his hand to indicate that I could speak.

"Look, forget about telling us where the King is," I said. "Can you tell us if there's a labyrinth anywhere around here?"

Relief washed over his face.

"So you know?" he said. "Oh, thank goodness. Follow me!"

Mark Antony looked like he was about to question me, but then seemed to change his mind and said nothing. Eleni, Mark Antony and I followed Quentin into the castle and down into its deepest depths.

"We simply couldn't understand it!" he gabbled as he hurried ahead. "The King has been so frail lately, and when he said he was going to live in the labyrinth we all thought he'd gone mad! Of course, he's never been the same since those awful Romans took his daughter during the siege." He looked up and saw Mark Antony's grim expression. "No offence!" he added with a weak giggle.

As we left the upper windowed levels behind, it grew very dark. Quentin lit a torch and the flames lit up the narrow corridors in a really creepy way. I wished I'd brought the omnilume. Mark Antony's eyes were flicking left and right, and his hand stayed over his sword's hilt. I could tell that he suspected we were walking into a trap.

Finally we arrived at a small room, in which there was nothing but a single trapdoor in the floor. Quentin opened it and handed us the torch.

"I can't go any further," he said. "The King ordered us to stay away. He said that someone would come who asked about the labyrinth, and we should show them the entrance. I suppose that's you!"

He gave his weak giggle again, and I could see Mark Antony's hand gripping the hilt of his sword. I think Quentin noticed it too, because he wished us luck and scurried off into the darkness.

"Ready?" I asked my companions.

"Ready," they replied together.

A ladder led down from the trapdoor to a passage below. It was carved out of the earth, and it was just the right height for Eleni and me, but

Mark Antony had to stoop. We hurried along the passageway. It smelled damp and was mega cold. I was starting to shiver when I saw a light ahead.

"Check it out!" I whispered.

We crept forward, swords drawn. The passage made a sharp bend and then opened out into a chamber, where a fire was crackling in the centre. A thin, grey old man was sitting beside it, warming his hands.

"Your Majesty!" said Mark Antony.

I took a step forward, but before I could say a word, Eleni flung herself forward and threw herself into the man's arms.

"Father!" she cried.

"Eleni!" he replied.

Tears rolled down the King's face as he hugged her. I felt as if someone had taken my brain and made custard out of it. What was going on?

When they finally finished hugging, the King explained that Eleni was his long-lost daughter. She had been in Rome so long that she had forgotten her life in Gaul. Eleni was a princess!

It was incredible, but there was more to come. When I told the King my name, he stood up and hugged me with shaky arms.

"I have been waiting for you, Will," he said. "I cannot explain it, but I have something to give you. Titus has been helping me to guard it until you arrived. I could trust no one else."

I gawped at him, questions fizzing inside me.

- How could the King of Gaul know that I was coming?
- Where was Titus?
- What was he guarding?
- What did they want me to do?
- Why did they want me to do it?

This was TOO weird!!

With his arm around Eleni, leaning on her, the old King led us through a complicated maze.

At last we saw another light ahead of us, and the King turned to me with a smile.

"You have returned my daughter to me," he said. "I can never thank you enough."

He shook my hand, then urged me on towards the light. The passage opened out into a long, narrow bunker, where another fire was crackling. The bunker was lined with weird-looking bricks.

"It's gold!" Mark Antony suddenly exclaimed. "There must be a fortune in here!"

"It's a ransom," said the King. "I had been collecting it to bribe my daughter's kidnappers to return her to me. But you have rescued her and brought her back instead. Please, take this gold back to Caesar and thank him for returning my little girl to me."

I had expected Titus to be a mighty Roman general – a grown-up – not a boy. It was weird – I felt like we already knew each other.

Two hours later, the place was bustling with action. Mark Antony was overseeing his best soldiers as they packed the gold ready for the journey back to Rome. Eleni was talking at double speed, telling her dad about all the things that had happened to her, and I was finally able to talk to Titus alone.

"I couldn't take the gold to Rome by myself," he explained. "I was sure to meet barbarians – I needed the protection of an army. But I also needed someone I could trust not to take the gold for himself. I wasn't even sure about Mark Antony – he's pretty ambitious. I needed another Solvit Adventurer."

"But how did you know that?" I said. "How did

you know that there were other Solvit Adventurers and that I would be turning up in Rome?"

Titus looked around cautiously and leaned closer to me.

"Someone's been leaving me letters," he whispered. "And the letters told me all about you!"

CHAPTER TEN
ALL ROADS LEAD TO ROME

After the army had rested and our stocks had been replenished, we prepared to head back to Rome with the gold. Eleni came to say goodbye to me, and I grinned when I saw her. She was wearing a flowing silk dress with jewels in her hair. She looked like a different person from the slave girl in rags who I had met in the arena. I suddenly realized that I had revealed my secrets to a very important person.

"Take care on your way back to Rome," she said. "I hope that you make it home as safely as I have. And I hope you find your parents one day, just like me."

We hugged goodbye, and as she pressed her cheek to mine, she added in a soft whisper, "Your secret is safe with me."

I smiled at her as we broke apart and then shook hands with the King.

"Have a safe journey," he said. "I wish you well."

The journey back to Rome seemed to last forever, and I loved it. I used the time to perfect my sword-fighting skills, and – of course – to chat to Titus about being an Adventurer. We got on so well, it felt as if I had known him all my life.

Titus was really interested to learn that I didn't

yet know what my special Adventuring skill was. His was warfare, and he was brilliant at it. He taught me a whole bunch of things about strategy, combat and politics, and I told him about the future, and Morph, and about my missing parents.

Our journey seemed to be gobbling up time. We were distracted along the way by a barbarian battle here or a civil war there, and the weeks stretched into months and then into years. We had no modern way of tracking time, but I reckon I must have almost been a teenager by the time we finally glimpsed the Seven Hills of Rome in the distance. I had grown out of all my clothes, and I was so used to wearing the Roman military tunic that I couldn't imagine sticking my legs into jeans again!

"This time tomorrow, we'll be in Rome," said Titus as we sat in his tent that evening.

"Then it's time I returned this to you," I said.

I reached into my battered, dusty old backpack and pulled out the sword. It seemed like centuries since I had lifted it down from the wall of Grandpa's attic.

"Just don't forget, this has to end up in Solvit Hall one day," I said.

I had told him everything and he understood that it all depended on me finding that sword in the attic in the future. Titus took it in his hand and smiled at me.

"One day I'll hand it down to my children as an heirloom," he replied. "It'll reach you again, don't worry."

We entered Rome like heroes! Messengers had been sent ahead to announce our return, and the streets were filled with crowds of people waving banners and shouting our names. Children stood on rooftops and scattered rose petals down on our heads, and men and women rushed up to press small gifts into our hands. It seemed as if the news of the gold had reached everyone's ears.

It was wonderful, but I couldn't help noticing that a lot of the houses were more crumbling than ever, and the streets were bumpy and dirty. Even the Temple of Castor and Pollux looked dull and uncared for.

"First stop, Caesar's palace," said Mark Antony. "I imagine he will be waiting for us with open arms."

I wouldn't have thought it possible, but Caesar seemed to have grown even fatter and more spoiled than before. When we laid the bricks of gold in front of him, I thought he might actually start drooling. He ordered everyone except us out of the chamber, and then skipped around the bricks,

nearly tripping over his toga.

"Gold!" he gasped. "Glorious gold!" He rubbed his hands together and chuckled. "I shall shoe all my horses in gold! I'll have a throne made of it and a bed and a new laurel crown and –"

"Caesar!" exclaimed Mark Antony.

He made the word sound like a whip crack. Caesar jumped and turned to stare at him.

"This city is the heart of the Empire," said Mark Antony, "but it looks like a filthy village. We need new buildings and new temples."

Caesar's mouth had fallen open, and so had mine. At this rate, Mark Antony was going to talk himself straight into the arena!

But Mark Antony continued. "We need to make Rome the jewel in the crown of our Empire! There's enough gold here to repair the whole city."

RESPECT!

He jabbed Caesar in the chest and sent him crashing into his ornate chair. Caesar stared up at Mark Antony, and for about ten seconds no one moved or spoke. Then...

"Whatever you say, Mark Antony!" Caesar squeaked.

Success!

Titus tugged on my cloak and drew me aside.

"I need to talk to you in private!" he whispered.

We crossed to the far end of the chamber, and then he drew a sheet of parchment out of his pouch. His eyes were as round as marbles, and expressions of excitement and sadness seemed to be struggling with each other on his face.

"I've had another letter," he said. "I found it just before we came in here."

"What does it say?" I asked, feeling weirdly worried.

Titus put his hand on my shoulder and spoke softly.

"It says that you should activate Morph," he said. "It's time for you to go home."

CHAPTER ELEVEN
HOME AGAIN

When Morph arrived in my bedroom at Solvit Hall, I clattered down the spiral stairs in my heavy Roman boots and burst into the kitchen, where Grandpa was unpacking some shopping. He looked up at me and raised his eyebrows.

"Interesting outfit, Henry."

"Grandpa, it's so good to see you!"

I threw my arms around him and gave him a mammoth hug.

"Ouch!" he complained. "Your wrist cuffs are digging into my back! Whatever is the matter with you?"

"I'm just so pleased to see you!" His lack of enthusiasm was mega weird. "Haven't you missed me?"

"I haven't had time to miss you!" Grandpa said huffily. "I've only just read your friend's note telling me that you're going off on an Adventure. Why haven't you gone yet? And what is that peculiar smell?"

I collapsed onto a kitchen chair.

"But...I've been gone for years!"

Understanding swept across Grandpa's face. "Time travel has no rules, Will. Hours can turn into days, months, even years. And our usual rules of getting older don't apply either. So you might have had a birthday or two while you were away but you're still the same age now. Time travel follows its own set of rules, just like Morph."

My mouth fell open.

"How old am I going to end up being if I'm a time traveller all my life?" I demanded in shock.

Grandpa didn't answer my question. He reached into one of the shopping bags and pulled out a packet of coconut-and-jam biscuits. I've no idea where he finds these things.

"Here, have a biscuit," he said. "Time travel's bound to disagree with you sooner or later."

I looked at the table. My revision books and the remains of Grandpa's snacks were still there. I had been gone almost no time at all.

I opened my reference book and it fell open at a paragraph about Caesar:

Many of Julius Caesar's ideas made him popular with soldiers and civilians. People trusted him and called him 'Father of the Homeland'.

Caesar reorganized the army and cleared Rome's enormous debts. He spread the country's wealth to ensure the poor had enough to eat.

Caesar also had coins made with his face on them and even had statues of himself dressed up to look like statues of the gods.

I thought of the little man I had met and raised my eyebrows. Caesar must have really smartened up his act after I left. And Mark Antony definitely had something to do with that.

I flicked on through the book, glancing at chapters about politics, the army, society and the Empire. The last time I had looked at this book, it had seemed impossible to know it all in time for the test on Monday. Now I not only knew it all – I knew a lot more than the writer of the textbook ever would!

I thought about Titus, and wondered what had happened to him. Had he stayed in Rome? Had he lived a happy life? I wished that I could see him again. In that chamber in Caesar's palace, I had been in such a rush to get home that I hadn't even said a proper goodbye.

Suddenly I remembered something. The mile-long driveway of Solvit Hall was lined with statues of my ancestors! I leaped to my feet and rushed out of the house.

Skidding over the gravel, I raced down the line of serious-looking faces until I came to a man dressed in the same sort of outfit that I was wearing. His right hand was resting on his sword, and his expression was serious but kind. I peered into the stone face, and I could see the boy I had known in the man he would become. Underneath the statue, these words were carved into the plinth:

TITUS SOLVIT
BC 55 - AD 35
WARFARE EXPERT

I reached out my hand and placed it on the stone shoulder, just as he had done to me less than thirty minutes ago.

"Hey Titus," I said. "Good to see you again."

By the time I'd had a shower, pulled on some jeans and a T-shirt, and had something to eat, I was feeling a lot more normal. I pulled my SurfM8 from my backpack (which was still covered in dust from ancient Rome) and sent an IM to Zoe.

Wilz: I'm back!

SingaporeSista: Already? That was quick!

Wilz: Not 4 me! I've been gone yrs!

SingaporeSista: No way!

Wilz: Way! Tell u abt it on Mon. U havin fun with ur dad?

SingaporeSista: Awesome 2 c him! He's got a load of new gadgets – can't w8 2 show u.

Wilz: Sounds gr8! C u Mon?

SingaporeSista: C u then!

My backpack needed to see the inside of a washing machine fast. I emptied it and checked all the pockets. Tucked into a zipped compartment I found the key to the attic.

I wonder...I thought. I walked up to the attic and slowly opened the door. Gleaming on the wall, looking as if it had never moved, was Titus's sword. I smiled and was about to close the door again when I saw a white envelope on the dusty floor of the attic. I hurried forward and picked it up.

WHAT'S THE EASIEST WAY TO DEFINE TIME TRAVEL? THROW AN ALARM CLOCK AT THE WALL!

CONGRATULATIONS ON ANOTHER SUCCESSFUL ADVENTURE, WILL! YOU'VE DONE THE SOLVITS PROUD.

YOUR NEXT ADVENTURE IS NOT FAR AWAY.
LOOK FOR YOUR MOTHER IN THE PAST.
LOOK FOR YOUR FATHER IN THE FUTURE.

I locked the attic again and went back to my bedroom, wondering when my next Adventure was coming and where it would take me. The latest letter showed that there were still tons of things I didn't know – including what my special skill was.

I could hardly wait to find out the answers to all my questions. But whatever mysteries still had to be solved, I knew one thing for certain: I was going to ace that Roman history test!

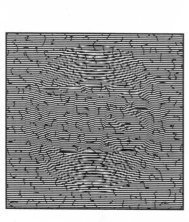

You'll never guess what was waiting for me in my school locker today. Yep, you guessed it...a letter.

WHAT SUBJECT ARE SNAKES GOOD AT IN SCHOOL?
HISSSTORY!

YOU'LL MEET A LOT OF SNAKES ON YOUR NEXT
ADVENTURE... IN FACT, YOUR NEXT ADVENTURE
WILL BE THE MOST DANGEROUS, TESTING, BRUTAL
ADVENTURE YET.

YOU NEED TO PREPARE YOURSELF FOR
WHAT'S AHEAD.

HERE ARE SOME CLUES THAT WILL HELP YOU FIGURE OUT WHICH ANCIENT CULTURE YOU'LL BE VISITING...

- THEY LIKE TO SACRIFICE HUMANS
- THEY PLAY FOOTBALL WITH THEIR ENEMIES' HEADS
- THEY'RE SURROUNDED BY JUNGLES
- THEY'VE BUILT MAGNIFICENT TEMPLES

AND ONE MORE THING, WILL...

THEY KNOW YOU'RE COMING.

OTHER BOOKS IN THE SERIES